HiT entertainment

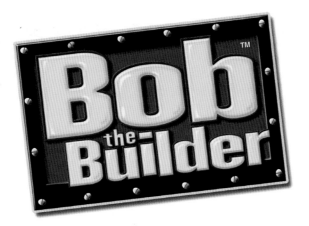

Bob the Builder™

WATCH ME DRAW
BOB'S BUSY DAY

Step-by-step drawing illustrations by Elizabeth T. Gilbert

Safety first! When Bob works up high, he places safety cones and warning signs nearby to keep everyone safe. Muck's extra helpful when Bob needs a helping hand!

DRAW A SAFETY CONE!

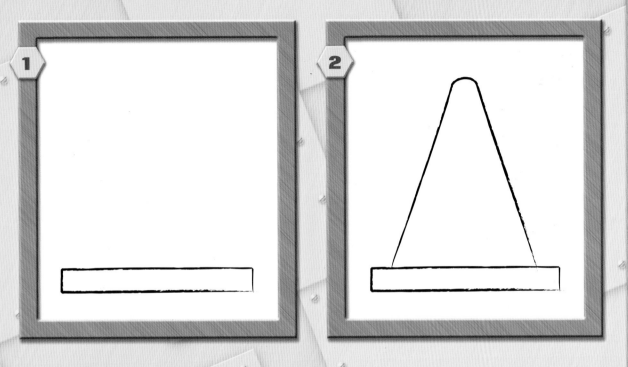

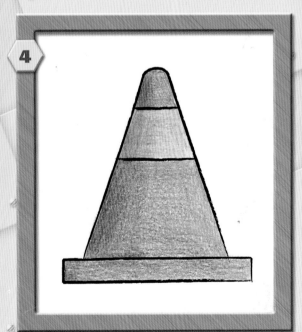

When you finish your drawing,
place the warning sign sticker on the opposite page!

Oh such a perfect day! When the weather is nice, Bob loves to work outside. It can be building a garden path for a friend or installing solar panels. There's nothing like flowers to brighten up your day!

DRAW A FLOWER!

When you finish your drawing,
place the tool belt sticker on the opposite page!

Sometimes the top is the place to start! Today Bob and the Can-Do Crew are starting a renovation project with the roof. Next come new windows and a coat of paint. Then this house will be as good as new!

DRAW A HOUSE!

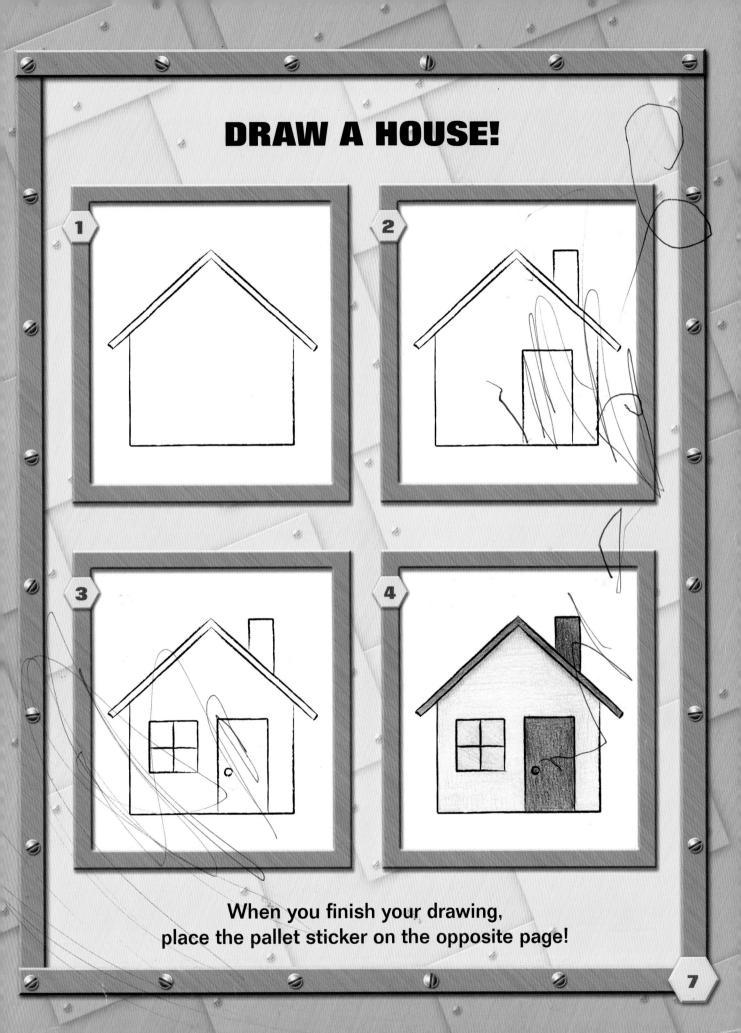

When you finish your drawing,
place the pallet sticker on the opposite page!

With friends like Lofty and Roley, even big jobs are simple. Lofty's ready to lift and Roley's ready to roll! Can we build it? "Yes we can!" Do you see Wendy peeking out of the shed?

DRAW THE MOUNTAINS!

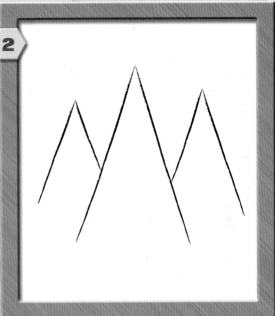

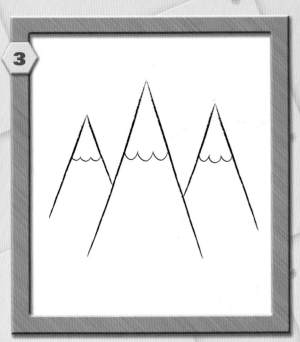

When you finish your drawing,
place the Bob sticker on the opposite page!

The Can-Do Crew is ready for a new project. At the shore or in the mountains, they work together to get the job done! Roley, Dizzy, Lofty, Scoop and Muck are all ready to roll. Who else is ready?

DRAW A LIGHTHOUSE!

When you finish your drawing,
place the Scrambler sticker on the opposite page!

Every project starts with a plan! Bob reviews every detail with the Machine Team. Sometimes they plan the next day's activities after the sun has gone down and it's dark outside.

DRAW A LANTERN!

When you finish your drawing,
place the Dizzy sticker on the opposite page!

Muck can carry big loads, but when friendly squirrels need to use the road, the heavy load can wait. Bob will look near and far to make sure all the squirrels get home.

DRAW A SQUIRREL!

When you finish your drawing,
place the tree sticker on the opposite page!

Even when he barks up the wrong tree, Scruffty is a valuable member of the team. He can always provide a laugh for the rest of the team! What is Scruffty running to now?

DRAW A TREE!

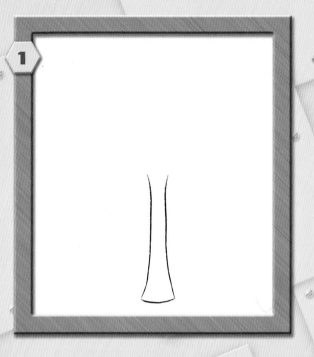

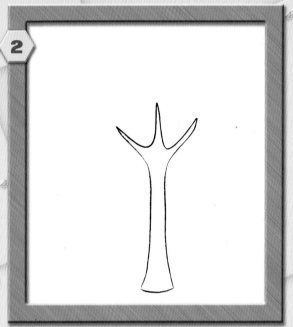

When you finish your drawing,
place the Scruffty sticker on the opposite page!

Bob the Builder and his friend, Wendy, use all kinds of tools to get their jobs done. Scruffty would like to help too, but that bone isn't a tool!

DRAW A WRENCH!

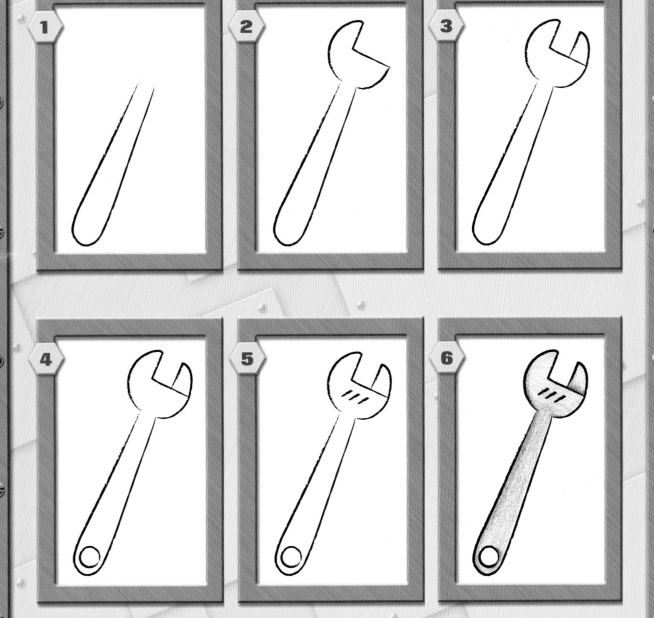

When you finish your drawing,
place the bucket sticker on the opposite page!

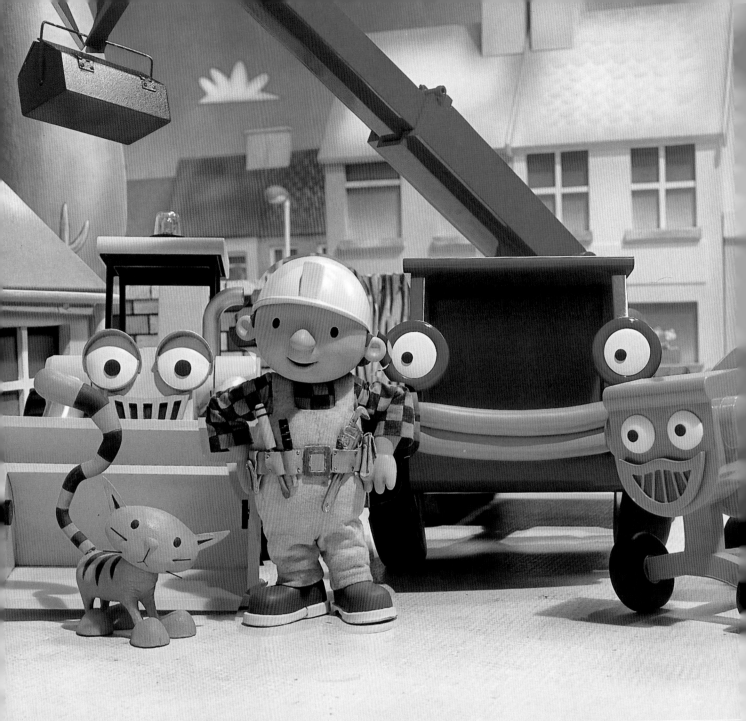

Bob's missing his toolbox! Dizzy doesn't have it. Scoop doesn't have it. Does Pilchard have it? Does Lofty have it?

DRAW A CAT!

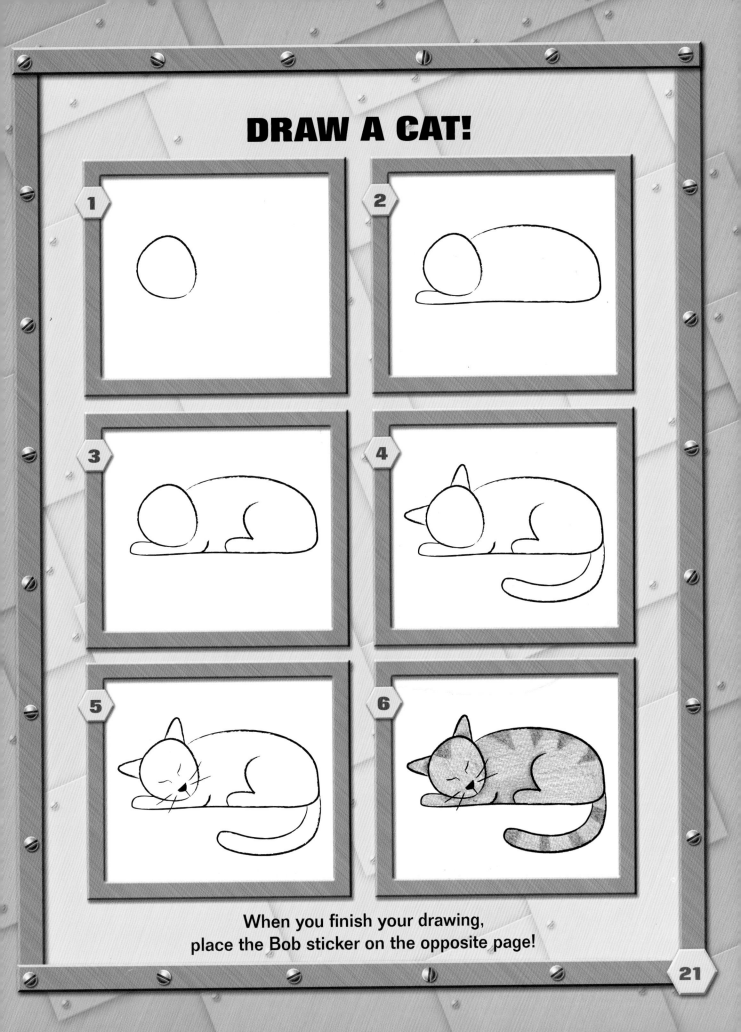

When you finish your drawing,
place the Bob sticker on the opposite page!

Packer collects, carries and delivers products all around the valley. When Bob sees some rabbits, Packer knows just what to do. He waits until they've moved along at their own pace.

DRAW A BUNNY!

When you finish your drawing,
place the bunnies sticker on the opposite page!

Congratulations!
You're a big help to the Can-Do Crew!